My Furry Foster Family

Truman the Dog

by Debbi Michiko Florence
illustrated by Melanie Demmer

PICTURE WINDOW BOOKS
a capstone imprint

Thank you to Jocelyn, at Save One Soul Animal Rescue, for her help
with research — DMF

My Furry Foster Family is published by
Picture Window Books, a Capstone imprint
1710 Roe Crest Drive, North Mankato, Minnesota 56003
www.capstonepub.com

Library of Congress Cataloging-in-Publication Data
Names: Florence, Debbi Michiko, author.
Title: Truman the dog / by Debbi Michiko Florence.
Description: North Mankato, Minnesota : Capstone Press, [2020] | Series:
My furry foster family | Audience: Age 5-7. | Audience: K to Grade 3.
Identifiers: LCCN 2019004134| ISBN 9781515844754 (library binding) |
ISBN 9781515845607 (paperback) | ISBN 9781515844792 (eBook PDF)
Subjects: LCSH: Dogs—Anecdotes—Juvenile literature. | Foster care of
animals—Juvenile literature.
Classification: LCC SF426.5 .F595 2020 | DDC 636.7—dc23
LC record available at https://lccn.loc.gov/2019004134

Designer: Lori Bye

Photo Credits: Mari Bolte, 66, 67, 68, 69; Melanie Demmer, 71; Roy Thomas, 70

Printed and bound in the United States of America.
092519   002751

Table of Contents

Dad
(Tim Takano)

Mom
(Cindy Takano)

Me
(Kaita Takano)

Eraser

Ollie

Hannah Miller, my best friend

Joss Lawrence, Happy Tails Rescue

CHAPTER 1

A Special Phone Call

I held a dog treat in my hand.
"Ollie, sit!" I said.

My happy dog wagged his tail and
sat down.

"Good boy!" I said. I tossed the
treat in the air. Ollie caught it in his
mouth. He crunched and crunched,
then he sniffed the floor for crumbs.
He didn't want to miss one.

"I think you got them all, Ollie!" I said, giggling.

"Kaita! I'm home!" a voice called. It was my mom.

Ollie and I ran to the kitchen. The tags on his collar jingled like little bells.

Mom had a pile of books on the table. She works at a bookstore. I love it because she gets me books about animals. When I grow up, I want to be a veterinarian. I'm going to be the best animal doctor ever!

"Are those books for me?" I asked.

"Yes," she said. "There's a book about cats, a book about birds, a book about dogs, and a book just about dachshunds, like our Ollie." She slid the books in front of me.

I gave her a big smile. "Oh, thank you, Mom!"

Yip! Yip! Yip! Ollie barked and ran to the back door.

"That must be Dad!" I said, running after Ollie.

Yip! Yip! Yip!

Dad walked in, bent down, and patted Ollie's head. He got hugs from Mom and me.

"Coming home to my family is my favorite thing," Dad said. "Hey, I have some good news!"

"What is it?" I asked.

Dad smiled, but he didn't say anything. He took off his jacket. He hung it on the hook. He put his backpack on the floor. He took off his shoes.

"Dad!" I said. "Come on. What is it?"

"Yes, stop teasing us," Mom said with a smile.

"OK, sit down at the table, and I'll tell you," he said.

We all sat down. Ollie curled up under my chair.

Dad grinned. "I got a phone call from Happy Tails Rescue," he said.

I peeked under my chair. "That's where we got Ollie," I said.

We had adopted Ollie from Happy Tails Rescue last year. The poor little dog had been found in a parking lot with no collar and no home. Happy Tails took him in. They rescue animals and help them find forever homes. I was so happy we became Ollie's forever home.

"What did Happy Tails Rescue say?" Mom asked.

I wiggled in my chair.

"They have a dog who needs a foster family," Dad said. "He needs love and a place to stay until he finds a forever home. And *we're* going to foster him!"

"Hooray!" I said.

"When?" Mom asked.

The doorbell rang. Ollie barked. *Yip! Yip! Yip!*

"Right now!" Dad said, jumping out of his chair.

Mom and I followed him to the front door. Mom scooped up Ollie in her arms.

It was Joss, the awesome lady from Happy Tails Rescue. "Hello, Takano family!" she said. "Thank you for agreeing to foster."

Ollie wagged his tail. I could tell he remembered Joss.

"Hello, Ollie!" Joss said, patting his head.

"Where is the dog?" I asked.

"Truman is in my truck," Joss said.

"Will Truman like Ollie?" I asked.

"Truman is friendly with other dogs," Joss said as we walked to her truck. "He is an older dog. He is a very sweet Labrador mix."

"What happened to his family?" I asked.

"Truman's family had to move far away. Sadly they couldn't take Truman with them," Joss said. "We will find him a wonderful new home and family."

When we got to the truck, Joss opened the door and grabbed the leash. A black dog jumped out. He was bigger than Ollie. He stood close against Joss' legs, like he was trying to hide.

"He is beautiful," I said.

Truman looked at me and blinked. His tongue rolled out. His thick tail thumped against Joss.

"Look at that. I think he likes you, Kaita," Joss said.

I liked Truman too!

CHAPTER 2

Hello, Truman!

Before Joss left she gave us a bag
of Truman's toys. She gave us a crate
too. We put the crate in my parents'
bedroom. Truman would sleep there.
Ollie already slept with me in my room
every night.

After dinner I worked on a puzzle
with my parents. I like puzzles. They
are fun to put together. Ollie curled up
on my lap. Truman sat by the door.

"He seems sad," I said. "Maybe he wants to go home."

"This *is* his home now," Dad said. "It will take time for him to feel safe with us. He doesn't know us yet."

I dug into Truman's bag of toys and found a stuffed lamb. I tossed it. It landed at his feet with a *plop.*

Truman sniffed the toy a little but didn't move.

I got a tennis ball. I waved it in front of his face and rolled it past him. "Get the ball, Truman!" I said.

Truman watched the ball but didn't move.

Ollie did, though. He shot after the ball like a rocket. *Yip! Yip! Yip!*

Truman's ears went up. He wagged his tail and barked. *Woof! Woof!*

Ollie ran past him, and Truman followed right behind. And just like that, the two dogs became friends.

***

The next day Ollie and Truman played tag. Ollie chased Truman from the living room to the kitchen, up the hall, and into my room. Truman chased Ollie out of my room, down the hall, into the kitchen, and to the living room.

Back and forth the dogs ran. They barked nonstop.

Dad got a little upset. He was trying to talk on the phone for work.

"Come on, you two!" I said. "Let's play quietly in my room."

Ollie, Truman, and I went to my room and sat on the floor. I pulled a bright-yellow rubber ducky from Truman's bag of toys. Truman wiggled and whined.

"Want your ducky?" I asked him.

Truman wagged his tail and licked my hand. I gave him the toy. He squeaked it a couple times.

Playing tag had made the dogs tired. I lifted Ollie onto my bed. He curled up. Truman wanted to get on my bed too, but I said no. Joss had told us to keep Truman off the furniture. His forever family might have a "no furniture" rule.

I got Truman's dog bed from his crate and put it on the floor.

"You can take a nap over here, Truman," I said.

Truman sniffed his bed, snorting from end to end. When he had sniffed every inch, he stepped onto the bed. He turned in a circle three times, plopped down, and curled up tight. With a sigh he fell asleep.

"Good dog," I said.

Ollie watched me tiptoe to the door. I put my finger to my lips. "Shh!" I whispered. He stood and pawed at the air. He wanted to be picked up. I walked back to my bed and got him, then closed the door behind us.

While Truman napped I sat at the kitchen table with my sketchbook. It already had lots of Ollie drawings in it: Ollie in his alligator costume, Ollie chasing a ball, Ollie lying on his back with a big, full belly . . .

Now I started drawing Truman. I wanted a way to remember him after he found a forever home. I drew three pictures: one of him sitting, one of him with his rubber ducky, and one of him sleeping on his bed.

Yip! Yip! Yip! Ollie barked and ran to the back door.

"Mom's home!" I said.

Mom walked into the kitchen with her book bag. "Hello, Ollie!" she said. "Hi, Kaita! How is Truman doing?"

"Great!" I said. "He and Ollie
played tag all morning. Truman took
a nap. He's in my room."

"Perfect. Let's take them for a
good, long walk," Mom said.

I ran to get Truman, but when I
opened my bedroom door—Oh no!
It looked like a blizzard had blown
through my room!

Ripped paper covered everything
like snowflakes. My trash can was
tipped over. My desk chair was too.
Truman was sitting in the middle of
it all, his dog bed shredded to bits.

"Truman!" I shouted.

Ollie came running and stopped
in the doorway. *Yip! Yip! Yip!*

I don't always have the neatest bedroom. Mom usually has to tell me to clean up. But this was a *disaster!*

Ollie looked at the mess Truman had made, then he sneezed.

Truman dipped his head. He tucked back his ears. He looked very sorry.

"Oh, dear," Mom said when she saw my room. "Truman found trouble, didn't he?"

"Yes, he did," I said.

Ollie sneezed again and backed up into the hallway.

I went over to Truman. I held his head in my hands. "Did you think we forgot about you in here? Huh?" I asked. "I'm so sorry. You're OK, Truman. Don't worry."

"Kaita, I'll take the dogs for a walk," Mom said. "You start cleaning your room. If you're still working on it when we get back, I'll help you finish."

I nodded. "Thanks, Mom."

"Ollie, time for a walk! You too, Truman!" Mom called, heading back to the kitchen. Ollie followed Mom, and Truman followed Ollie.

Mom and Dad had said that it would take time to learn how to foster pets. I sure learned a good lesson that day: Never leave a foster dog alone in your room!

CHAPTER 3

Truman Finds Trouble

I wasn't the only one learning how to foster a pet. Mom and Dad were learning too. Every day brought new lessons.

"Oh, Truman," Mom said, looking sadly at her ripped book bag. "You found trouble."

"Oh, Truman," Dad said, looking at a chewed shoe. "You found trouble."

"Oh, Truman *and Ollie*," I said, looking at a torn, empty box of dog treats. "You found trouble." I gave both dogs' bellies a quick rub. "Well, at least you two are happy."

Dad, Mom, and I quickly learned our lessons. When we couldn't watch Truman, we put him in his crate. We made sure there was nothing he could rip or chew on the floor. Unlike short little Ollie, Truman could reach the countertop when he stood on his hind legs. So we cleared off everything!

Our daily routine went like this: In the morning, before Dad took me to school, I fed Ollie and Truman. After school Mom and I took the dogs for a walk. During homework time Ollie slept on one side of me. Truman slept on the other. After dinner we played. At bedtime, when Dad read a story to me, Ollie and Truman listened too.

The five of us were a happy, furry foster family.

***

A couple weeks later, Mom and I came home to a big surprise.

Yip! Yip! Yip! Ollie greeted us at the door like he always did. But then—

Woof! Woof!

"Truman! How did you get out of your crate?" I asked.

"Maybe I forgot to close the gate," Mom said.

Woof! Woof! Truman rose on his hind legs and licked my face.

I laughed and gently pushed him away. After I did that, my hand felt sticky. Why? Before I could figure that out, Ollie ran into the other room. He usually followed me when I got home. Something wasn't right.

Truman wagged his tail. I saw a yogurt lid stuck to his back. The fur on his head looked matted and oily. Someone had found trouble!

"Mom?" I said, looking around, my eyes wide.

"Oh, my goodness!" Mom cried. "What is all of this?"

The trash can was tipped over. Dirty wrappers, broken eggshells, banana peels, and other trash covered the kitchen floor.

Truman nudged my legs. Potato chip crumbs dusted his nose.

"Eww! You stink!" I cried.

Truman's tongue hung out, like he was smiling and pleased with himself. He ran to the middle of the floor and rolled around in the trash, back and forth. The eggshells crunched. He slid on the banana peels. He waved all four paws in the air. He sure was a happy dog!

"Oh, Truman," Mom said. "You found trouble! You need a bath."

I hurried to the bathroom and filled the tub with warm water. When Truman heard the water running, he ran into my room. He tried to hide under the bed. He did not want a bath!

Ollie poked his nose into my room. He smelled Truman, backed up, and ran down the hall. I didn't blame him. Truman was stinking up my room fast.

"Truman, it's OK. We just want to get you cleaned up," I said. "Baths are *fun*." I talked in a calm voice while Mom hooked his leash to his collar.

We walked Truman to the bathroom, and he sat down in the doorway. That was it. He wouldn't go any farther. Mom pulled. I pushed. The dog would not move.

"I don't get it. I thought Truman would like water because he's part Labrador retriever," I said.

"Every dog is different," Mom said.

That's when I got an idea. I ran to Truman's crate and got his rubber ducky. Holding the toy over his head, I said, "Truman, get your ducky!" I tossed the toy into the tub. *Splash!*

Truman's ears perked up. He leaped. *SPLASH!* Truman was in the tub!

Mom and I quickly soaped him up.
He sat still, with his toy in his mouth.
We scrubbed. We rubbed. We rinsed.
Soon Truman was clean again.

He jumped out of the tub. *Shake!
Shake! Shake!* He shook the water from
his fur. Now Mom and I were all wet!
We started laughing.

"You are a good dog, Truman,"
I said, hugging him.

CHAPTER 4

Old Friends, New Friends

Ollie, Truman, and I had great fun together. We loved to go on walks and play fetch. The three of us made a good team.

I started to wonder if my family could be Truman's forever home.

One day my best friend, Hannah, came over. She liked Ollie a lot, but she was nervous to meet Truman.

"Don't worry. He is one terrific dog," I said to her.

Hannah and I went to my room. *Yip! Yip! Yip!* Ollie loved Hannah. He wiggled and squirmed like a puppy in her lap.

I ran to my parents' room and got Truman from his crate. He barked and licked my face. *Woof! Woof!* Before I could stop him, he ran down the hall toward my room.

"Truman, wait for me!" I laughed.

When Truman got to my room, he stopped in the doorway. He saw Hannah sitting on my bed. He did not go in. I walked past him and sat next to Hannah and Ollie.

Truman stood and looked at us for a long time. He wagged his tail but stayed in the hall.

"It's OK, Truman," I said. "This is Hannah. She's my best friend."

Truman sat down.

"Look. Ollie loves Hannah," I said. Ollie wagged his tail and licked Hannah's face.

Truman slowly stepped into my room. He crept to my side and stuck close to my leg, away from Hannah. He kept watching her.

"He can be shy with new people," I said. "It takes a little time for him to feel safe." I remembered when Truman first met my family.

"Truman, I want to be your friend," Hannah said. "Do you want to be mine?" She held out her hand, palm up. She stayed very still.

Truman carefully leaned across me. He sniffed her hand.

Hannah smiled. Truman thumped his tail.

"Good boy," she said.

Woof! Woof!

Truman licked Hannah's hand. She giggled. "Truman, you *are* a terrific dog," she said.

"I told you!" I said.

I was so glad all four of us were friends now! We grabbed some toys and went to the backyard to play.

"Kaita, you really like Truman, don't you?" Hannah asked.

"I do!" I said. "He's the perfect fit for my family!"

Hannah smiled, but she looked a little sad too. "Too bad he can't stay here forever. It's going to be hard to say goodbye."

I didn't want to think about that.

***

Dad made my favorite dinner that night: hamburgers with fried eggs. Right after we sat down at the table, Mom said, "Guess what?"

"What?" I asked.

"Joss called me today. She might have a family for Truman," she said with a smile.

"That's great!" Dad said.

I looked down at the floor. On one side of my chair was Ollie. On the other side was Truman. What would it be like when Truman wasn't here anymore? I felt a tug in my heart— and a lump in my throat.

"So what happens next?" I asked. I leaned down and patted Truman's head. I rubbed his ears.

"Joss will make sure the family is good for Truman," Mom said. "After that the family will call me or your dad. They'll ask us questions about Truman, and we'll tell them everything about him. If they think he sounds like the right dog for them, they will come to our house to meet him."

"Be sure to tell them he needs to be crated," I said. "Tell them he eats things that are not food, like trash and blankets. Remember what he did to your book bag? And Dad's shoe? Remember the mess in my room?"

"Yes, we will tell them the truth about Truman," Dad said. "We want Truman to find his forever home."

"Be sure to tell them he doesn't like baths. Tell them he is shy with new people," I said.

Mom put down her hamburger and looked at me. "We will also be sure to tell them all the *terrific* things about him too. He loves other dogs. He knows how to sit, come, stay, and lie down. He plays fetch. And he is very loving."

"Are you sad about Truman leaving, Kaita?" Dad asked.

I didn't feel like eating anymore, even if it was my favorite dinner. I looked down at my plate and nodded.

"Honey, we talked about this, remember?" Mom said.

"I know, I know," I said. "Truman's just so . . ."

"By fostering we are helping a lot of animals, instead of just one or two that we would be able to adopt," Mom continued.

Dad reached over and rubbed my shoulder. "I know it's tough, Kaita," he said. "You've done a great job with Truman! He's had a safe, loving home away from home with us. We taught him good manners. We also learned what makes him special, so we can help him find a good match with a family."

Mom's eyes got a little wet. She smiled and said, "No matter what happens, Truman will always have a place in your heart. He'll have one in your dad's heart and my heart too."

I knew all of this. Of course I wanted to help animals, but I had fallen in love with Truman. How could I say goodbye?

CHAPTER 5

A Terrific Dog

The family that Joss told us about was not the right fit for Truman. They called and talked to Dad. The family loved to go fishing, and they wanted a dog to take to the lake. Dad told them he wasn't sure Truman would like the lake. Truman hated baths. To Truman a lake would seem like one big bathtub!

A day later a man called and talked to Mom. He wanted a quiet house dog, one he could leave in his house while he went to work. Mom told him that Truman sometimes chewed things like blankets or rugs when he was alone. He wouldn't be a good fit for the man.

Another week went by.

"Joss says that older dogs are harder to find homes for. Many people want puppies," Mom said.

"Truman is housebroken. He's already trained. That makes things *easier* for a family," I said.

Dad nodded. "True," he said. "Does this mean you aren't sad anymore about finding a home for Truman?"

I was still a little sad about Truman leaving, but I was sadder that nobody wanted to adopt him. He was a good dog. He deserved a forever family.

Finally, four days later, Mom had good news. "Mr. and Mrs. Garcia and their son, Ben, are coming to the house on Saturday to meet Truman," she said.

"Did you tell them everything?" I asked. "Did you tell them that Truman is terrific, but that sometimes he finds trouble too?"

"I did. They thought his antics were cute," Mom said.

I crossed my fingers. I loved having Truman here with us. But I wanted him to find his own home.

On Saturday morning I cleaned my room. I gathered all of Truman's toys and put them in his toy bag. Dad put Truman's bed next to the bag by the front door. We didn't know if this family would be a good fit. We hoped they would be.

The doorbell rang.

Yip! Yip! Yip! Woof! Woof!

I put Ollie in my room. I didn't want him to distract the Garcia family from Truman.

Mr. Garcia was tall. He smiled a lot. Mrs. Garcia wore jeans and a T-shirt with a picture of a dog on it. Ben was older than me, almost a teenager. The minute he saw Truman, he kneeled down.

Truman hid behind my mom.

I looked at Ben. I was worried that he would be upset, but he just smiled. I kneeled down too. "It's OK, Truman. These people want to meet you," I said.

Truman peeked around my mom's legs and looked at me. Then, wagging his tail, he walked right over to Ben and licked his cheek! Ben laughed.

"He is beautiful," Mr. Garcia said.

Truman went to Mrs. Garcia and sat down in front of her. "What a good boy!" she said, patting his head.

"He is terrific," Ben said, turning to me. "Your dad said he sometimes gets into trouble. I do too!"

"It looks like you and Truman will become best friends," I said.

"I hope so," Ben said.

"I think Truman will be perfect for our family," Mrs. Garcia said. "Can we take him home?"

I handed Truman's leash to Ben. Mr. and Mrs. Garcia gathered Truman's things. I let Ollie out of my room so he could say goodbye.

Right before it was time for him to leave, I hugged Truman, tight. "Have a wonderful life with your new family," I whispered in his ear. He licked me one last time. Mom, Dad, Ollie, and I watched the Garcia family and Truman drive away. Truman looked very happy.

"How are you doing, Kaita? OK?" Mom asked.

"I think so," I said. "I'm a little sad, but mostly happy."

Yip! Yip! Yip! Ollie crawled onto my lap and nuzzled my ear. I was happy he had found his forever home with us. I was happy Truman had found his forever home with Ben too.

***

Life at my house went back to its normal routine. Every morning I fed Ollie his breakfast. Every afternoon after school, Mom and I took him for a walk. Every evening he sat next to my chair as I did my homework. Every night he curled up on my bed to sleep.

Two weeks later Dad showed me an email from Mrs. Garcia. She said that they all loved Truman. Ben and Truman went to the park every day. Attached to the email was a picture of Truman with his rubber ducky in his mouth. He was sitting on Ben's bed. I guess they didn't have a rule about no dogs on the furniture!

Later that night, while I was doing a puzzle, Ollie ran to the back door. *Yip! Yip! Yip!* Mom was home from the bookstore.

"Oh, Kaita! Guess what?" Mom said excitedly.

"What?" I asked.

"We have another foster pet coming!" she said.

"Really? Hooray!" I cried.

I jumped, then started dancing with Ollie. All kinds of thoughts spun in my head. What kind of animal would we get? Another dog? A cat? Something more unusual, like a snake or a rabbit? I couldn't wait to find out. I was ready to help another animal find its forever home!

Think About It!

1. How does Truman tell Kaita that the rubber ducky is his favorite toy?
2. How are Ollie and Truman different from each other? Give three examples.
3. Do you think Truman is a terrific dog? Why or why not?

Draw It! Write It!

1. Kaita likes to draw. What is your favorite animal? Draw a picture of it.
2. Kaita worries that Truman might not find his forever home. Write a short newspaper ad that tells readers why they should adopt Truman.

Glossary

adopt—to take and raise as one's own

antics—playful or funny acts

crate—a cage

dachshund—a type of dog with a long body and short legs

distract—to draw attention from something

foster—to give care and a safe home for a short time

Labrador retriever—a type of strong, medium-sized dog often used for hunting

routine—a set of tasks done in a set order

veterinarian—a doctor trained to take care of animals; also called a vet

Fact or Fiction:
Who Is Kaita?

Kaita Takano is the main character of the
My Furry Foster Family series.

Did you know that there is a real-life Kaita?
Just like the Kaita in the series, she has a
miniature dachshund
named Ollie and
fosters animals
with her family.

The Kaita in this
book is fictional—that
means "made up" or
"imaginary." A writer
of fiction makes up
things to tell a story.

Nonfiction is based
on fact (true, real
things). There is nothing made up in
nonfiction. Kaita Takano likes to read
lots of nonfiction books about animals
so she can learn about them.

Eraser

Story Kaita and Real-Life Kaita are different in many ways.

Story Kaita is 8 years old and in third grade. She is Japanese American. She has no pets other than her dog, Ollie.

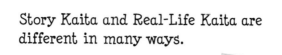

Real-Life Kaita is 11 years old and in fifth grade. She is half Korean American, half European American. In addition to her dog Ollie, Kaita has many other pets. She has another dog, three cats, and a pony!

Story Kaita enjoys putting together jigsaw puzzles and drawing animals. Real-Life Kaita enjoys knitting, sewing, and playing video games with Ollie.

The Kaitas are alike in some ways too. They both love to draw and read. Story Kaita reads nonfiction books about animals. Real-Life Kaita enjoys graphic novels best, but she also likes to read nonfiction. Neither Kaita has brothers or sisters. They both live with their mom and dad.

CAT CARE
BIRD FACTS
DOG·BREEDS

And the biggest thing the two Kaitas share? Nothing makes them happier than helping pets find their forever homes!

Wait! The two Kaitas do share one more, very important thing: They think you're awesome for reading this story!

About the Author

Debbi Michiko Florence writes books for children in her writing studio, The Word Nest. She is an animal lover with a degree in zoology and has worked at a pet store, the Humane Society, a raptor rehabilitation center, and a zoo. She is the author of two chapter book series: Jasmine Toguchi (FSG) and Dorothy & Toto (Picture Window Books). A third-generation Japanese American and a native Californian, Debbi now lives in Connecticut with her husband, a rescue dog, a bunny, and two ducks.

About the Illustrator

Melanie Demmer is an illustrator and designer based out of Los Angeles, California. Originally from Michigan, she graduated with a BFA in illustration from the College for Creative Studies and has been creating artwork for various apparel, animation, and publishing projects ever since. When she isn't making art, Melanie enjoys writing, spending time in the great outdoors, iced tea, scary movies, and taking naps with her cat, Pepper.

Go on all four fun, furry foster adventures!

Apple and Annie, the Hamster Duo

Betty the Bearded Dragon

Buttons the Kitten

Truman the Dog

Only from Capstone!